# Cowee Girls

## and the
## Solar
## Eclipse

# By Claire Suminski
# and Molly Suminski

First Edition
ISBN 9780998589923


Library of Congress Control Number (LCCN):  2017944976


Published by Red Press Co.

Redpressco.com

Cowee Mountain Valley Farm is in the "Path of Totality" of the 2017 Great American Solar Eclipse

Cowee Mountain Valley Farm
**RUF RUF 5**
NORTH CAROLINA

Farmer Joe, Ruby, Annie, Cowee Sam and Buttercup set off in the red truck to deliver invitations to the eclipse party.

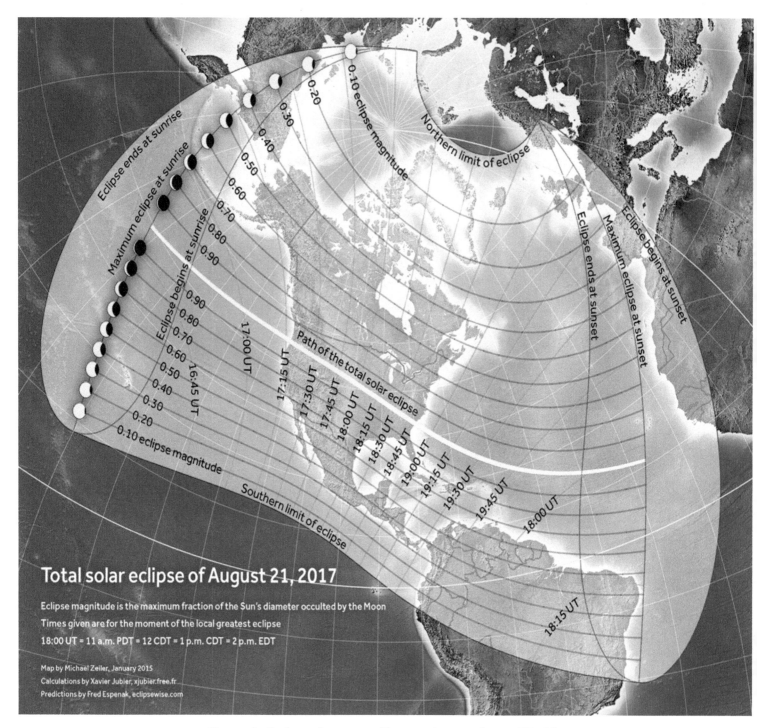

Total solar eclipse of August 21, 2017

Eclipse magnitude is the maximum fraction of the Sun's diameter occulted by the Moon

Times given are for the moment of the local greatest eclipse

18:00 UT = 11 a.m. PDT = 12 CDT = 1 p.m. CDT = 2 p.m. EDT

Map by Michael Zeiler, January 2015
Calculations by Xavier Jubier, xjubier.free.fr
Predictions by Fred Espenak, eclipsewise.com

Special thanks to: GreatAmericanEclipse
GreatAmericanEclipse.com for permission to use their amazing maps
and graphics

Map and analysis by Michael Zeiler, May 2017

On Monday, August 21st, 2017, the moon will pass in front of the sun, casting its shadow across all of North America. Nowhere will the total eclipse be more prevalent than in Macon County, North Carolina, where the duration of total eclipse will last an amazing 2 minutes, 30 seconds. Molly and Claire Suminski continue the wonderful adventures of Cowee Sam. This latest book will take you on a journey about the eclipse as only Cowee Sam can. Even though this is a book for children, many adults will also find this book to be enjoyable and educational. Thank you, Molly and Claire, for bringing us Cowee Sam and The Solar Eclipse.

I would also like to extend a special thank you to the entire Suminski family. Their continued involvement and service to our community makes it a better place to live, work, and play.

Ronnie Beale, Vice Chairman
Macon County Board of County Commissioners

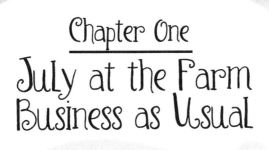

# Chapter One
## July at the Farm
## Business as Usual

The sun shone brightly on Cowee Mountain Valley Farm. The chickens were laying beautiful white, tan, brown, and blue eggs. Farmer Joe was harvesting the vegetables for his wife Ruby to put up for the winter. The blueberries were ripe for the picking. In many ways, it was business as usual at the farm, except, The Great American Solar Eclipse was less than a month away!

Farmer Joe finished walking the fence line with his Great Pyrenees dog, Sam.
Cowee Sam, was the faithful guardian dog of Cowee Mountain Valley Farm. With Sam on duty, the chickens were safe from the raccoons, foxes and hawks that made their homes in this beautiful mountain valley.
Sam's ears perked up at the familiar sound of the US mail truck approaching the farm.

3

Mail-carrier Dorothy pulled up, waving out her window. Her blue heeler, Stamp, had a letter in his mouth and held it out for Joe.

"Special Delivery for the Franklin Family, Farmer Joe. It looks like you got a letter from your granddaughter!"

A big smile stretched across Farmer Joe's face as he took the envelope from Stamp and patted his head.

"Annie might be coming to visit soon. I think I'll go read this letter with Ruby. Thanks, Dorothy."

Farmer Joe and Cowee Sam hurry up to the orchard to find Ruby and Buttercup.

"I've got a letter from Annie here!" said Joe, handing the envelope to Ruby. She gave it a quick look over, and a big smile cames across her face.

"Having our granddaughter here during the eclipse is going to make it even more exciting! Let's go in the house and read the letter again and make a plan. Come on Buttercup."

Dear Grandma and Grandpa,

Things are abuzz at my house! Everyone is rushing around and packing. My Mom and Dad are off to Morocco in a few days to work on a newly uncovered fortress. They are excited to break in their new archeological brushes and try couscous for the first time. I am so happy because that means I'll get to come stay with you for a whole month!

Mom and I were looking at the calendar to see when I should come visit you and it reminded me of the science project I did last year in school. I learned all about solar eclipses and talked to my class about them. I even found out when the next one would be. Well, there's a total solar eclipse coming up in a couple weeks, and we'll be able to see it from your farm! These things don't happen very often, so I am really excited to see it. Maybe we can have a viewing party!

I love you, and I'll see you soon!
.Annie

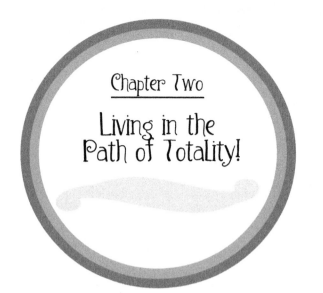

All around Macon County and through the Cowee Valley, excitement was building for the solar eclipse. A few days later Annie arrived. Since Cowee Mountain Valley Farm was her home away from home, she gave her grandparents quick hugs and then headed for the pasture with Buttercup to see all of the animals. This visit was going to be special. The farm would be in the center path of the eclipse!

Serving Macon County and the Cowee Valley Area

# NIKWASI NEWS

World - Business - Finance - Lifestyle - Travel - Sport - Weather     Est - 1965

THE WORLDS BEST SELLING NATIONAL NEWSPAPER     Monday 5th June

Issue: 240104

First Edition

## Franklin, NC is in the "Path of Totality" for the Solar Eclipse!

This is the first TOTAL SOLAR ECLIPSE ABLE TO BE SEEN FROM THE SOUTHEASTERN UNITED STATES SINCE THE SOLAR ECLIPSE OF MARCH 7 1970. TOTAL SOLAR ECLIPSE WILL NOT HAPPEN IN OUR AREA AGAIN UNTIL... THIS ONE!

The Great American Eclipse
of August 21, 2017

North Carolina

Cullowhee

Franklin

2 min 10 sec
2 min 20 sec
2 min 30 sec
2 min 32 sec
2 min 34 sec
2 min 36 sec
2 min 38 sec
2 min 39 sec

COWEE MOUNTAINS

Map courtesy of :
GreatAmericanEclipse.com

9

Later that afternoon, Annie walked into the living room holding a large book with several papers and photos poking out of the sides.

"I have something to show you" she said, sitting down on the couch between Ruby and Farmer Joe.

"My teacher gave me this book when I was working on my Solar Eclipse project last year. She went all the way to Australia once to see a total solar eclipse, and she said that it was the most wonderful thing she had ever seen!"

Annie opened the book to a page with detailed illustrations of the sun, moon, and earth. Farmer Joe and Ruby leaned in to see the page, and Sam poked his head over the top of the book to get a peak.

"This is a model of a solar eclipse," said Annie, pointing to the illustration.

"It shows the moon passing between the sun and the earth. When that happens, the moon's shadow is cast onto the earth and it blocks out the sun. If you are standing on the ground in the exact area where the shadow falls, you'll be able to see the eclipse!"

# Chapter 5: The Solar Eclipse

A solar eclipse is an eclipse occurring when the Sun, Moon and Earth are on a distinct line, with the Moon being in the middle. Seen from the Earth, the Moon is in front of the Sun and because of this part, or all of the light of the Sun is hidden by the Moon. It can make it seem that the Sun has disappeared, or that a section of the Sun missing.

## SOLAR ECLIPSE
SUN, MOON, AND EARTH
LINE UP, WITH THE MOON IN THE MIDDLE

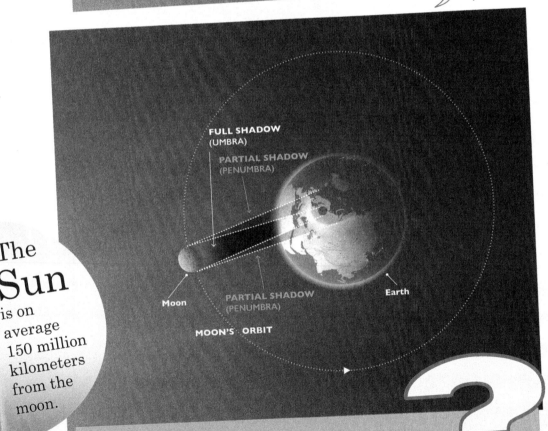

**FULL SHADOW** (UMBRA)

**PARTIAL SHADOW** (PENUMBRA)

**PARTIAL SHADOW** (PENUMBRA)

**Moon**

**Earth**

**MOON'S ORBIT**

The **Sun** is on average 150 million kilometers from the moon.

What makes it seem like the Sun disappears?

During a full Solar Eclipse it will appear that the sun is dissappearing in stages. In the above photos, you can see through a series of photos how the sun disappears in stag...

Annie turned the page as she explained the event and pointed to a series of photos of an eclipse.

"My teacher says that if you are in the path of the eclipse, you can see a black circle slowly move over the sun. When it is totally covered, it looks as if the sun has disappeared, and there is just a ring of soft light around the black disc. But, since the moon is always moving around the earth, the total eclipse only lasts for a few minutes. Then, the shadow slowly moves away, and the sun reappears.

My teacher had to wear special glasses to protect her eyes when she went to see the eclipse in Australia. When the sun was completely covered, she took the glasses off. She said it was like nighttime for a few minutes, but then the sun started to peak out, and it was very important to put her glasses back on, so she could continue watching."

Ruby marveled at the photos and handed Annie a cup of tea and a plate of delicious Solar Eclipse cookies that they had made earlier in the day.

"What a wonderful sight, and how exciting that we are living in the path of totality! I can't wait to see it in a few weeks."

Farmer Joe agreed. "I am so proud of you for learning all about this, Annie. I think having a viewing party like you suggested is a great idea."

"That's right!" Ruby said. "I was talking to Dorothy the other day, and she said that there hadn't been an eclipse visible in the United States since 1979, and she heard that there would not be another one for many years to come! This is a pretty rare event, and it's only right that we celebrate it!"

Later, the trio sat down for dinner to continue discussing the party with excitement in their eyes and tasty food in their bellies.

# Solar Eclipse Cookies

## Ingredients:

3/4 cup of Butter
2 cups of Sugar
2 well-beaten Eggs
1/2 cup Molasses
2 teaspoons of Vinegar
3-3/4 cups of plain Flour
1-1/2 teaspoons of Baking Soda
2-3 teaspoons Ginger
1/2 teaspoon of Cinnamon
1/4 teaspoon Cloves
Marshmallows

## Directions:

Cream Butter and Sugar,
Add Eggs, Molasses & Vinegar
Sift Dry Ingredients and add to creamed mixture.
Form into 3/4 inch balls and bake on parchment paper lined cookie sheet for _**12 minutes in a 325 degree oven.**_
Cut Marshmallow in half and put cut side down on almost baked cookies. Return to the oven for about _**two minutes.**_

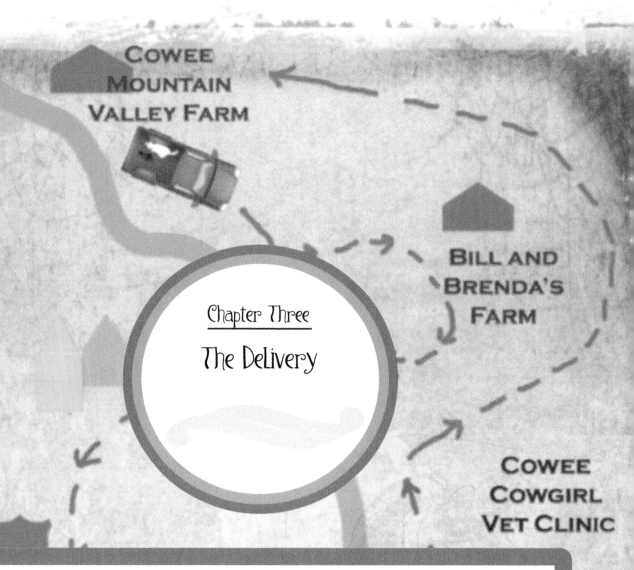

COWEE
MOUNTAIN
VALLEY FARM

BILL AND
BRENDA'S
FARM

COWEE
COWGIRL
VET CLINIC

## Chapter Three

### The Delivery

Farmer Joe announced, "I'll put Buttercup's pack on and she can carry the invitations. We can all deliver them!"

Farmer Joe, Ruby, Annie and the two dogs, set off in the red farm truck to deliver the invitations. Their first stop was Windy Knolls Farm, home of Bill and Brenda, and their Border Collies, Joy, Hope, and Luke.

INVITATION DELIVERY PLAN

Cowee Mountain Valley Farm

**RUF RUF 5**

NORTH CAROLINA

## Chapter Four
## Dogs at Work

As Farmer Joe's red truck entered Windy Knolls Farm, Annie looked out in the field and saw Bill Coburn working with his Border Collies. The dogs were herding the geese towards the neighboring pasture, closely following Bill's commands. He sent out a series of whistles, signaling for Joy to run after a goose that had broken away from the gaggle. Joy responded immediately, dashing after the wayward one and guiding it back towards the group. When the last of the geese had been lead into the east pasture, Brenda closed the gate, and the collie returned to Bill's side.

Annie, watching as the dogs worked, turned to Farmer Joe and asked, "What would Uncle Bill do without his Border Collies?"

"Border Collies are great working dogs. They have been helping farmers herd their sheep, geese, and other animals for ages. Bill and Brenda have put a lot of work into training their dogs Joy, Hope, and Luke. In fact, right now, they are preparing the dogs for competitions at the Highland Games." Farmer Joe told Annie as Bill, Brenda, and their dogs walked over to them.

Annie told their neighbors all about the Solar Eclipse, and Sam pulled an invitation out of Buttercup's pack and placed it in Brenda's hand.

Bill said, "You can count on us to be there!"

Brenda added, in her lovely southern drawl, "Why, I can bring some of my shepherd's pie."

They said their goodbyes and got back into the truck, then crossed the bridge to go into town to visit

As they pulled up to the fire station, they saw the line of fire engines in the parking lot. At the end of the line was a big yellow school bus, which stuck out against the flame-red trucks.

"Dave must be hosting another field trip," Ruby remarked, "the kids from the elementary school love his after school program."

Farmer Joe, Ruby, Annie, Cowee Sam, and Buttercup proceeded into the firehouse in time to catch the end of Dave's presentation. He and his Dalmation, Smoke, were standing in front of the firetruck, accompanied by a display of fire gear, hoses, and pictures of old firetrucks. Twenty or so children sat crisscross applesauce on the floor in front of them, with big eyes and wide smiles stretched across their faces. They were attentive as Dave wrapped up his speech.

"So remember kids, if you ever find yourself on fire, STOP, DROP, and ROLL."

As he said the words, stop, drop, and roll, Smoke stiffened, dropped to the floor, and rolled several times.

The kids cheered!

The students packed up and filed into their bus while Annie got out another invitation and handed it to Dave.

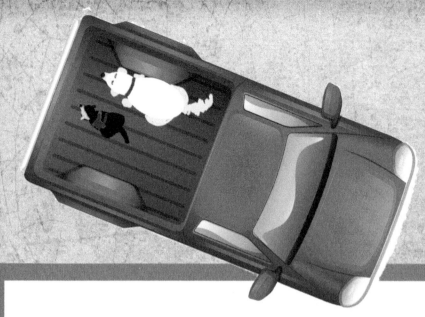

The last stop of the day was the Sheriff's Department to see Sheriff Robbie, who was outside working with his two K-9 dogs, a beautiful Blood Hound named Duchess and a sweet Plott Hound named Rex.

He looked over the invitation and said, "I will plan on bringing Duchess and Rex and would love to bring the family, too. I will ask my wife, Marci and our kids, Mason and McKayla to make some homemade dog biscuits to share at the celebration. All of the dogs will enjoy them!"

Before they left, Annie asked, "Sheriff Robbie, how do Duchess and Rex know what to do?"

Sheriff Robbie responded, "I take them to Canine Search and Rescue classes and then we practice regularly at home. Duchess is more experienced. Rex has a great nose for finding lost victims. He has just started his training."

Farmer Joe reminded them that it was time to head back to the farm for evening chores, and they said their farewells. Tomorrow would be a big day at Cowee Mountain Valley Farm. They would be seeing a total eclipse of the sun!

As their red truck pulled into the driveway, they saw Dr. Jessica Scruggs, their local large animal farm veterinarian. She and her therapy dog, Heart, were getting out of her "Cowee Cowgirl" truck. Dr. Jessica always seemed to know the right time to stop and check on their goats, hogs and of course, Sam. Farmer Joe and Ruby often remarked how hard it would be if they had to bring all of their animals to Dr. Jessica's office. It was a good thing that she made farm visits!

Last year, Heart had been hit by a car and lost the use of her front legs, so Dr. Jessica carried her in a back pack, especially made for dogs. Heart was very good at calming down patients and people.

Annie ran over and put an invitation in the Cowee Cowgirl's truck. Then they all headed into the pasture to check on the Mama goat named Jubilation, that would soon be giving birth to another kid. These were exciting times on the farm!

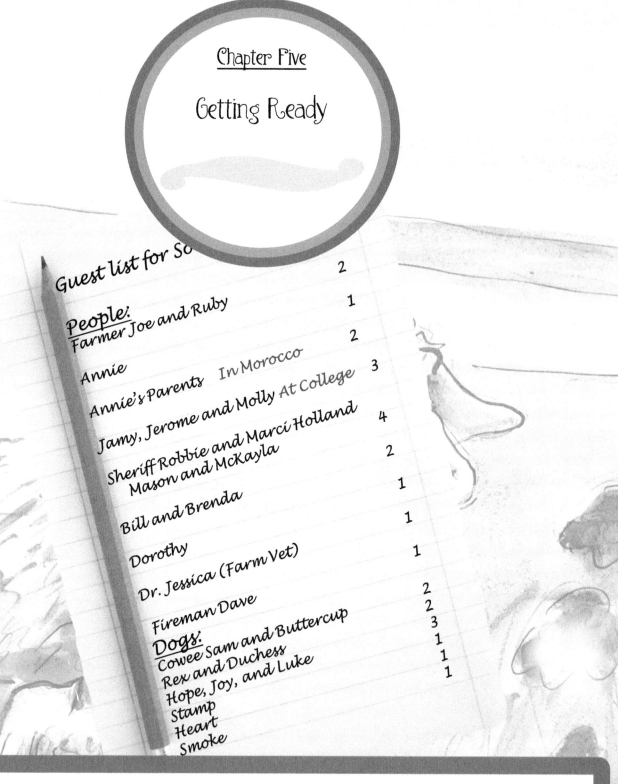

Guest list for So

**People:**
Farmer Joe and Ruby   2
Annie   1
Annie's Parents   In Morocco   2
Jamy, Jerome and Molly  At College  3
Sheriff Robbie and Marci Holland  4
Mason and McKayla  2
Bill and Brenda  1
Dorothy  1
Dr. Jessica (Farm Vet)  1
Fireman Dave  2

**Dogs:**
Cowee Sam and Buttercup  2
Rex and Duchess  3
Hope, Joy, and Luke  1
Stamp  1
Heart  1
Smoke  1

After the evening chores were done and the last dish from supper was dried and put away, Farmer Joe and Ruby and Annie sat out on the porch and went over the invitation list.

Early the next morning the farm radio went off and Ruby picked up the receiver and heard Dr. Jessica's voice. She was at the Sheriff's department and was radioing over to check on Jubilation, the Mama goat.

"How is the Mama goat doing?"

"I will stop by later."

The morning of the solar eclipse, Farmer Joe and Annie could not find Mama Jubilation in the main pasture. Had she given birth yet? They suspected Jubilation might have gotten out of the fence and headed down by the river and into the North Pasture. Goats can be very good at getting in and out of fences!

Ruby was in the kitchen getting food ready for the party. Farmer Joe and Ruby and Annie got together to pray and ask for God's help in finding Jubilation. The guests would be arriving soon.

Farmer Joe said, "I think we better call in reinforcements to help with the search."

Sheriff Robbie and his dogs and Fireman Dave arrived early to help with the search. Farmer Joe gave the sheriff a blanket that Jubilation had laid on the night before and grabbed his rescue worker bag. The dogs took off, leading them in the direction of Martin's Landing and the nearby North Pasture.

# Our Solar Eclipse Party

# TO DO:

Find Jubilation!!!!......Sheriff Robbie
                                Duchess & Rex

Feed the animals
& collect eggs .............Farmer Joe and
                                Annie

Set up food table........Ruby, Dorothy,
                                & Stamp

Make Solar Eclipse Cookies...Annie and
                                Ruby

Make Shepherds Pie...........Brenda

Fill Kiddie Pool with water...Jessica
                                and Heart

Greet guests...........Sam and Buttercup

Pass out glasses.................Annie

Clean-up......................Everyone helps!

The utility company had been working down by the river replacing  wood pecker damaged power poles. As they entered the gate to the North Pasture, they heard Jubilation bleating wildly. Had she given birth to her kid?   Her desperate cries lead them to the answer. Duchess and Rex ran ahead and made it to Jubilation's side first, followed by Sheriff Robbie.

He hollered out, "Jubilation had her baby!"

Annie arrived next and knelt down, peering into a hole with Jubilation's newborn at the bottom!

Farmer Joe summed up the situation by  saying, "This wee little newborn kid has fallen down into a hole dug for one of the new power poles!   But we can get him out!"

Farmer Joe knelt down next to Annie and took her hand in his. "Annie, you are the only one of us skinny enough to go down and rescue this kid. He is only about six feet down, but too far for us to reach. We will put a rescue harness around your waist  to safely lower you into the hole. There is only one thing, you will have to hang upside down!  Do you think you can do it?" Annie nodded her head, and Farmer Joe went to work.

He and Fireman Dave fit the harness around Annie and slowly lowered her into the hole, head first.

33

Annie quickly grabbed the kid and yelled, "I've got him!"

Both Mother and kid were bleating up a storm by this time. Farmer Joe took him from Annie's arms and put him down by his Mama to nurse.

He said, " Job well done Granddaughter.  You will have quite a story to tell your parents, and  I want you to name this baby goat. Sheriff Robbie, Duchess, and Rex head up to the house to tell Ruby the good news!"

"It's almost time for the party!" Annie exclaimed. Farmer Joe and Annie lead the mother and kid back into the main pasture and Cowee Sam greeted them, eagerly sniffing the baby Angora.

Annie said to her Grandfather, " I have a great name for Jubilation's kid.  Let's name him 'Eclipse'!  After all, he was born on August 21, 2017, right here in Macon County, North Carolina, just in time for the total eclipse of the sun! "

## Chapter Six
### Gathering to Watch the Eclipse

 The guests started arriving for the party.  Ruby had laid out a table of snacks, fresh made lemonade, ice cold spring water, veggies with dip and some Solar Eclipse cookies.

Some of the dogs were cooling off in the kiddie pools.

As Ruby looked around at the joyful party of friends and neighbors gathered at Cowee Mountain Valley Farm, her heart was filled  with thankfulness.

God made the sun, moon and the stars. How amazing that in just a few minutes they would witness the moon passing in front of the sun and a total eclipse would happen.

The shadows were deepening around them.

As the sky darkened, a quietness settled around them.  Even the birds were quiet. The fireflies started their regularly scheduled evening light show, blinking off and on, thinking that night had fallen. The moon would totally cover the sun for  2 1/2  minutes, starting at 2:36 PM.

Farmer Joe kept close track of the time and at 2:35 he started the Countdown.

"60 seconds to go! The moon is moving into position!   Keep your glasses on until the moon  is all the way in place!"

This would be the experience of a life time.  The last 10 seconds everyone counted down together. "10-9-8-7-6-5-4-3-2-1"

Cowee Sam, followed by the other dogs, started howling at the moon!

At this very moment it was safe for them to take their special solar eclipse glasses off and see the eclipse in all of its splendor.

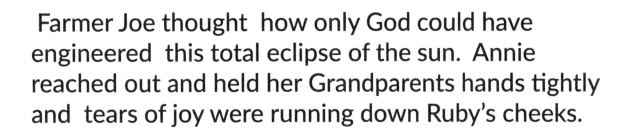

Farmer Joe thought  how only God could have engineered  this total eclipse of the sun.  Annie reached out and held her Grandparents hands tightly and  tears of joy were running down Ruby's cheeks.

The Great American Eclipse, August 21, 2017 was happening right now.  Amazing!  Ruff-Ruff!  Wow!

As the Sun began to show its glow once again, Annie and the others put their glasses back on. Their hearts were filled with amazement and joy at the sight they had just experienced.

# Glossary

**Angora Goat** (proper noun) a breed of domestic goat that grows long silky hair known as mohair

**Announce** (verb) to make known publicly or officially

**Approach** (verb) to come near or nearer to

**Archaeological** (adjective) of or relating to the study of historic or prehistoric people and their cultures through their artifacts and remains

**Attentive** (adjective) thoughtful of others

**Bleating** (verb) the cry of a sheep, goat, or calf.

**Bloodhound** (proper noun) a medium to large breed of dog that usually has black and tan fur, very long ears, loose skin, a great sense of smell raised to follow human scents.

**Blue Heeler** (proper noun) a breed of cattle dog raised to herd cattle by biting near their heels

**Border Collie** (proper noun) a breed of herding dog originally from the border of Scotland and England usually with black wavy fur with white fur around the neck, chest, face, feet, and tail raised for herding sheep and cattle

**Competition** (noun) a contest for some prize, honor, or advantage

**Couscous** (noun) a North African dish of steamed semolina usually served with vegetables and meat

**Crisscross Applesauce** (idiom) to sit with your legs folded; cross-legged

**Dalmatian** (proper noun) a breed of dog with short white fur with black or brown spots

**Dash** (verb) to move quickly; rush

**Deepen** (verb) to make or become darker

**Deliver** (verb) to carry and turn over to the intended recipient

**Desperate** (adjective) having an urgent need or desire

**Distinct** (adjective) distinguished as not being the same; specific or separate

**Eager** (adjective) impatiently longing

**Fire Engine** (noun) a vehicle used for firefighting

**Firefly** (noun) a type of nocturnal beetle that has a soft body with a light producing organ near the rear of the abdomen

**Firehouse** (noun) a building where fire engines and firefighters are housed

**For Ages** (idiom) a long period of time

**Fortress** (noun) a large fort or a group of forts

**Gaggle** (noun) a group of geese

**Great Pyrenees** (proper noun) a large breed of dog with a heavy white coat raised to herd or guard animals

**Guide** (verb) to force a person, object, or animal to move in a certain path

**Harvest** (verb) to gather

**Herd** (verb) to drive or lead cattle, sheep, etc.

**Host** (verb) to perform the duties of someone who entertains guests

**Illustration** (noun) a picture in a book or magazine

**Invitation** (noun) the written or spoken form with which a person's is asked to go somewhere

**Kid** (noun) a young goat

**Kilometer** (noun) a unit of measurement that Is equal to 1,000 meters

**Knelt** (verb) to go down or rest on your knees or one knee

**Mail-Carrier** (noun) a person who works for the post office who delivers mail

**Marvel** (verb) to wonder at or be curious about

**Morocco** (proper noun) a country in Northwest Africa

**Newborn** (noun) a recently born person or animal

**Nurse** (verb) to suckle

**Orchard** (noun) a group of trees

**Pasture** (noun) land covered with grass and other low plants suitable for grazing animals

**Path of Totality** (noun) the area on Earth where the Moon's shadow falls during a total solar eclipse

**Peek** (verb) to look or glance at quickly

**Penumbra** (noun) the partial shadow in a solar eclipse

**Plott Hound** (noun) a breed of dog that typically has brindle-colored fur raised to hunt bears and wild boars

**Prepare** (verb) to get ready

**Proceed** (verb) to move forward or carry on

**Rare** (adjective) coming or occurring far apart in time; unusual or uncommon

**Reinforcement** (noun) extra people or supplies to help

**Remark** (verb) to say casually

**Ripe for the Picking** (idiom) to be at the perfect stage to be used

**Series** (noun) a group of related things

**Several** (adjective) more than two, but fewer than many in number

**Shepherd's Pie** (noun) a baked dish of ground or diced meat with a crust of mashed potatoes

**Sheriff** (noun) a law-enforcement officer who is in charge of keeping the peace

**Solar Eclipse** (noun) the obstruction of the light of the sun by the moon being between the sun and the Earth

**Southern Drawl** (noun) the accent people who live in the Southern United States may speak with

**Suggest** (verb) to mention something for consideration

**Suspect** (verb) to believe something

**Trio** (noun) a group of three people

**Umbra** (noun) the full shadow during a solar eclipse

**Visible** (adjective) that which can be seen

**Wayward** (adjective) to drift away from the group

**Wrap Up** (idiom) to finish something up

# Fun Solar Eclipse Facts of the Day

## 97 days to the total solar eclipse!

### Eclipse fact of the day — 16 May

It is often said that animals display peculiar behavior during a total solar eclipse. Stories mention cows returning to the barn, roosters crowing, and more.

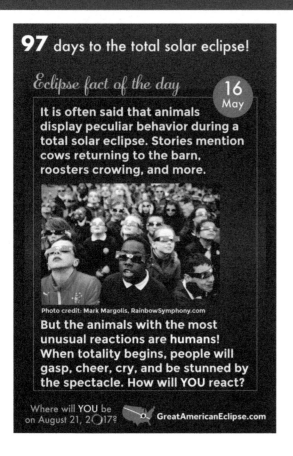

Photo credit: Mark Margolis, RainbowSymphony.com

But the animals with the most unusual reactions are humans! When totality begins, people will gasp, cheer, cry, and be stunned by the spectacle. How will YOU react?

Where will YOU be on August 21, 2017? — GreatAmericanEclipse.com

## 101 days to the total solar eclipse!

### Eclipse fact of the day — 12 May

These are the basic rules for safe viewing of the solar eclipse.

- If you are OUTSIDE the path of total solar eclipse, you must ALWAYS wear eclipse glasses to view the eclipsed Sun.

- If you are INSIDE the path of total solar eclipse, use eclipse glasses EXCEPT during the two minutes of so or total solar eclipse.

During the 1st partial stage of eclipse lasting about an hour, you must protect your vision with eclipse glasses or other safe method.

Take off eclipse glasses only during the 2 minutes or so of total solar eclipse.

During the 2nd partial stage of eclipse lasting about an hour, you must again protect your vision with eclipse glasses or other safe method.

Also, NEVER use eclipse glasses with binoculars or a telescope.

Where will YOU be on August 21, 2017? — GreatAmericanEclipse.com

## 112 days to the total solar eclipse!

### Eclipse fact of the day — 1 May

The 'Diamond Ring' of a total solar eclipse is the moment when totality begins or ends. A very small bead of sunshine enhances the breathtaking corona of the Sun.

Courtesy of Rick Fienberg, eclipse.aas.org

This is widely regarded as the peak sight of a total solar eclipse and you get two on August 21st. Unless of course, someone proposes to you on eclipse day!

Where will YOU be on August 21, 2017? — GreatAmericanEclipse.com

## 113 days to the total solar eclipse!

### Eclipse fact of the day — 30 April

"The thrill of a lifetime!" Not hyperbole, a total solar eclipse is nature's most spectacular sight.

This 1927 poster from the UK advertised rail travel to the eclipse. Today, people have much greater mobility and visitation will soar.

Where will YOU be on August 21, 2017? — GreatAmericanEclipse.com

## 117 days to the total solar eclipse!

### Eclipse fact of the day

**26 April**

How rare are total solar eclipses? Not very rare; totality occurs somewhere on Earth about every 16 months on average.

Fifty years of total solar eclipses from 2015 to 2065

However, totality visits a given spot on Earth about every 375 years on average. Most occur in remote regions of the planet.

Where will **YOU** be on August 21, 2017? **GreatAmericanEclipse.com**

## 125 days to the total solar eclipse!

### Eclipse fact of the day

**18 April**

The Moon's shadow has two components, umbra and penumbra.

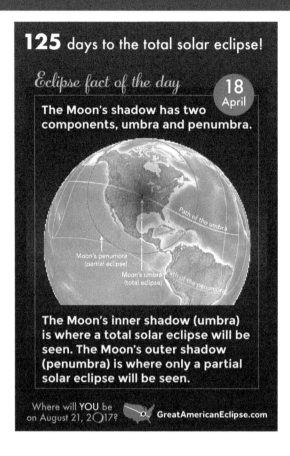

The Moon's inner shadow (umbra) is where a total solar eclipse will be seen. The Moon's outer shadow (penumbra) is where only a partial solar eclipse will be seen.

Where will **YOU** be on August 21, 2017? **GreatAmericanEclipse.com**

## 129 days to the total solar eclipse!

### Eclipse fact of the day

**14 April**

A remarkable citizen science project is planned across the nation on eclipse day called the Citizen Cate Experiment

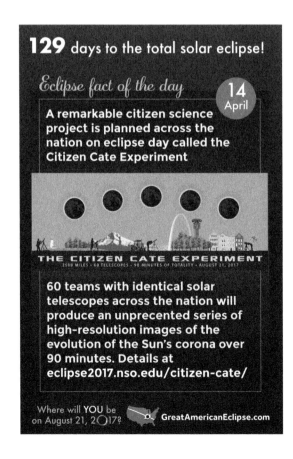

THE CITIZEN CATE EXPERIMENT
2500 MILES · 60 TELESCOPES · 90 MINUTES OF TOTALITY · AUGUST 21, 2017

60 teams with identical solar telescopes across the nation will produce an unprecented series of high-resolution images of the evolution of the Sun's corona over 90 minutes. Details at eclipse2017.nso.edu/citizen-cate/

Where will **YOU** be on August 21, 2017? **GreatAmericanEclipse.com**

## 142 days to the total solar eclipse!

### Eclipse fact of the day

**1 April**

While there is no pattern from one total solar eclipse to another, there is a pattern that repeats every 18 years, 10 days, and 8 hours called the Saros Cycle.

Saros Cycle 145

More at http://www.eclipsewise.com/solar/SEhelp/SEsaros.html

The previous total eclipse in this cycle passed over Europe in 1999 and the next visits Asia in 2035. Coincidentally, the 1999, 2017, and 2035 eclipses visit heavily populated areas.

Where will **YOU** be on August 21, 2017? **GreatAmericanEclipse.com**

# Working Dogs

Sometimes a dog owner needs a dog to be more than just a pet and needs the animal to assist them in a particular task or tasks. Some dogs are bred to have exacting traits that enable them to perform a job for their human companions. When this is the case the dog is known as a working dog.

There is a remarkable number of ways in which dogs can and do help humans. In the story "Cowee Sam and the Solar Eclipse" you met a few working dogs, like the Border Collies that help Bill and Brenda herd the geese and Fireman Dave's Dalmatian, Smoke, that helps him teach children about fire safety. Sheriff Robbie and the Sheriff's Department use their two hounds to do Search and Rescue.

Here are some ways that dogs have been utilized to help:

Livestock Guardian dogs: bred for the purpose of protecting livestock from predators.

Herding dogs: help gather cattle and other animals for ranchers and farmers and help guard the flocks and herds.

Service dogs: used to assist people with various disabilities

Therapy dogs: used to provide cheer and entertainment to those needing healing; others are also used to teach responsibility and to respond with love to help rehabilitate.

Rescue dogs: used to help people in difficult situations, they search for those lost whether in storms or in the wilderness, and oftentimes can reach where humans cannot.

There are also Sled dogs, Hunting dogs, Guard dogs, Detection dogs, Police dogs, Cancer Detection dogs, and War dogs. Dogs are pretty amazing aren't they?

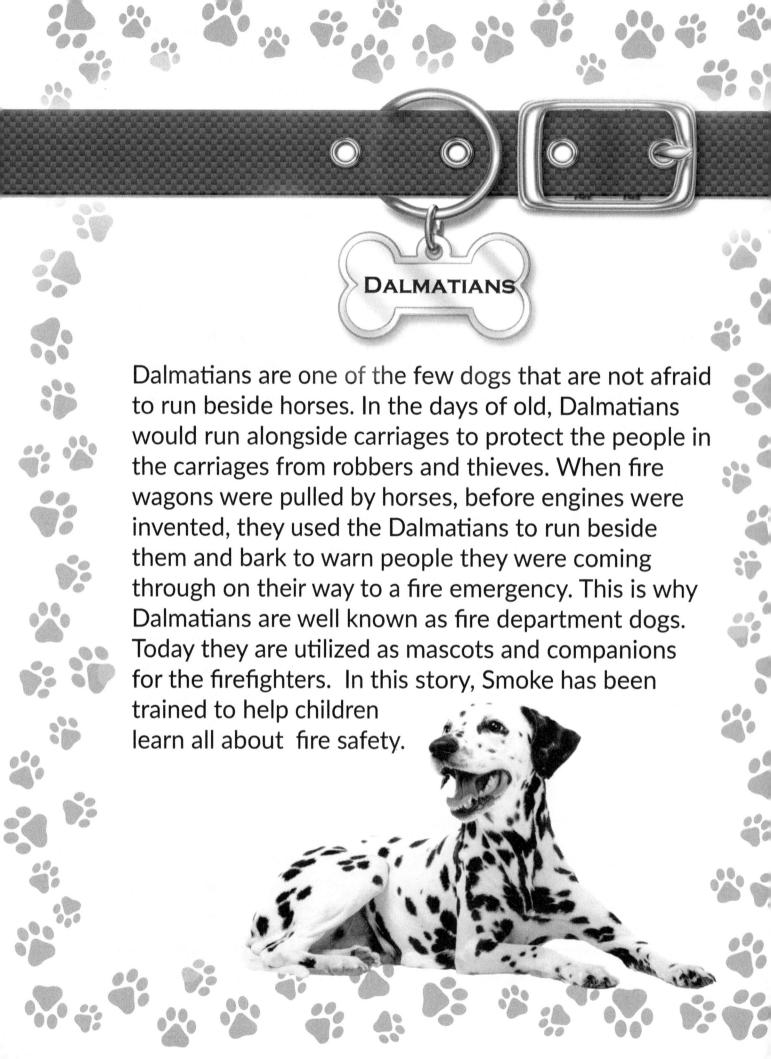

## DALMATIANS

Dalmatians are one of the few dogs that are not afraid to run beside horses. In the days of old, Dalmatians would run alongside carriages to protect the people in the carriages from robbers and thieves. When fire wagons were pulled by horses, before engines were invented, they used the Dalmatians to run beside them and bark to warn people they were coming through on their way to a fire emergency. This is why Dalmatians are well known as fire department dogs. Today they are utilized as mascots and companions for the firefighters.  In this story, Smoke has been trained to help children learn all about  fire safety.

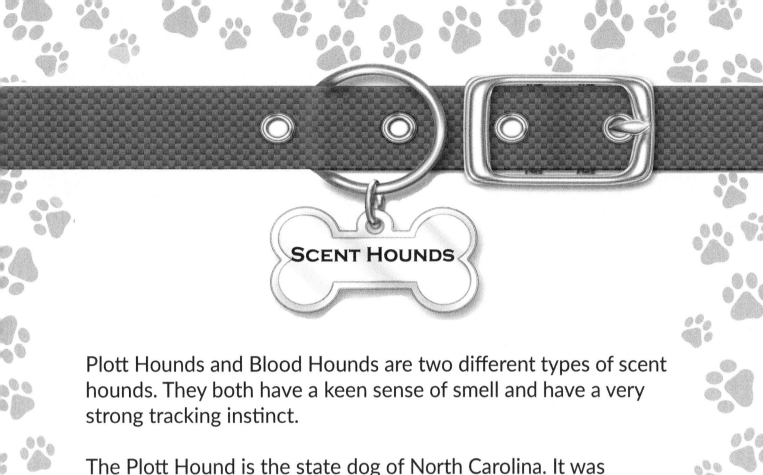

# SCENT HOUNDS

Plott Hounds and Blood Hounds are two different types of scent hounds. They both have a keen sense of smell and have a very strong tracking instinct.

The Plott Hound is the state dog of North Carolina. It was brought over from Europe and bred in the United States, right near where this story took place, in Western North Carolina.

The Blood Hound is actually physically built to follow scents. The chambers in the nose that identify smells are about forty times more sensitive than humans. Its long ears prevent the wind from diminishing the aroma when it's head is down tracking. It is believed that the folds in the skin serve to catch stray scent particules, reinforcing the dogs memory of the smell it is tracking.

# Solar Eclipse Word Scramble

Unscramble each of the clue words.
Take the letters that appear in the boxes with circles and unscramble them for the final message.

HATP FO TYTIALOT

SIOOCKE

DECHSUS

DOHRYTO

WIYDN KNLOLS RAFM

REISOUEFH

POTS PODR DAN RLLO

LODBUHNOOD

LUTJIIBOAN

CORSEH

ECLIPSA TOTALĂ DE SOARE
11 AUGUST 1999

ROMÂNIA 1100 L

1998    N. NOBILESCU    1998

TOTAL SOLAR ECLIPSE
1999 AUGUST 11

# Cowee Sam's Solar Eclipse
# Word Search

ABUZZ
ANGORA
ANNOUNCE
APPROACH
ARCHAEOLOGICAL
ATTENTIVE
BLEATING
BLOODHOUND
BLUE
COMPETITION
COUSCOUS
DALMATIAN
DASH
DESPERATE
DISTINCT
EAGER
ECLIPSE
FIRE
FIREHOUSE
FORTRESS
GOAT
GUIDE
HERD
HOUND
ILLUSTRATIONS
INVITATION
KID
KILOMETERS
KNELT
PASTURE
PLOTT
RARE
REINFORCEMENT
SOUTHERN

```
A P P R O A C H P A S T U R E
E E T C N I T S I D H N D H R
S A C F O R T R E S S E O S A
P N R N R E H T U O S M R A R
I W O O U T T O L P E E S D B
L A C I G O L O E A H C R A L
C G O A T N N R K D T R E L O
E A G E R A A N I N L O T M O
A B U Z Z T R K A U E F E A D
C O M P E T I T I O N N M T H
G N I T A E L B S H K I O I O
A T T E N T I V E U B E L A U
C O U S C O U S M N L R I N N
E S U O H E R I F E U L K S D
N O I T A T I V N I E D I U G
```

# Afterward

Molly and I have really enjoyed writing this book together. Molly has a great love of science and is majoring in Geology at nearby Western Carolina University. She worked on the science related aspects of this book.

Enrique Gomez, Associate professor of both Astronomy and Physics at Western Carolina University made the following comments on the WCU website.

"This will be the first total solar eclipse across the continental United States since 1979...

This is the first total solar eclipse visible in Cullowhee (near Macon County) since July 20, 1506. The next one, astronomers say, will occur October 17, 2153, making the 2017 eclipse a once-in-a-lifetime event."

We knew that we had to write a book about this very important event. This is what God's Word says:

> ## Genesis 1:16-18
> "And God made two great lights; the greater light to rule the day, and the lesser light to rule the night: he made the stars also.
> And God set them in the firmament of the heaven to give light upon the earth,
> And to rule over the day and over the night, and to divide the light from the darkness: and God saw that it was good."

Towards the end of the story it says that "Farmer Joe thought how only God could have engineered this total eclipse of the sun." That's what we think, too. Only God in all of his magnificence could have made the heavens and earth with such detail and love.

The Great American Eclipse website has been very generous in allowing us to use their beautiful graphics in this book. This quote comes from the "Eclipse basics" section on their website.

"The first fact to understand about solar eclipses is that they occur because of a remarkable cosmic coincidence:
The Sun is just about the same apparent size in our sky as the Moon. While the Sun is actually about 400 times larger in diameter than the Moon, the Moon is also about 400 times closer than the Sun. Therefore, the Sun and the Moon appear to be about the same size in our sky... We on Earth occupy a celestial sweet spot to witness this sight."

The website concludes that if there was life on other planets, the odds are very low that they would enjoy the same circumstance as we do on Earth. (In other words, Planet Earth may be the only planet in the whole firmament that has our special solar eclipse viewing capabilities!)

Our family enjoys writing these books very much. It is really God's Word and His love that are the center of our family and the heartbeat behind these books. May His ever abounding love and perfect peace be the heartbeat of each of your families, too.

*Philippians 4:20*
*"Now unto God and our Father be glory for ever and ever. Amen."*

We hope you had fun reading this book, and that you have many adventures of your own. The Suminski Family is going to keep on having adventures, and there are more Cowee Sam stories on the way!

Ever thankful for God's grace and love,
Claire and Molly Suminski
July 4, 2017

*Romans 10:9 "That if thou shalt confess with thy mouth the Lord Jesus, and shalt believe in thine heart that God raised him from the dead, thou shalt be saved."*

*Ephesians 2:8 "For by grace are ye saved through faith; and that not of yourselves: it is the gift of God."*

Ros Webb is a children's book illustrator. She has been illustrating children's books for close to a decade. She developed her own style as a children's book artist following the birth of her first daughter and the publication of her picture book "*The Big Sleepy Bear and the Pink Flamingos*". Ros lives in the Irish mountains and is greatly inspired by her three children, four dogs and five cats. She has worked extensively with authors from across the globe and is continually inspired by their imagination and story telling.

# Meet the Graphic Designer for the Cowee Sam Series

Susan Swedlund is an artist that lives most of the year in Beloit, Wisconsin. Recently she and her husband have been blessed to become part-time residents in Franklin, North Carolina.

Susan studied and received her Art degree at Washburn University in Topeka, Kansas. Along with being a Graphic Designer, Susan is a clay artisit and owns the business Potter Sister. While in Franklin she frequently teaches classes at Cowee Pottery School.

She and her husband, Glen, have fallen in love with the Cowee Valley and always enjoy seeing Cowee Sam when they walk their dog, April.

# About the Authors

Claire Suminski lives in a small Mountain community in Western North Carolina. Her husband and four children run a family business and have built a small hobby farm together. After twenty years of Home Schooling, Claire thought it might be rewarding to share family stories and adventures with more children and help fuel in them their love of learning.

Molly Suminski is a Junior at Western Carolina University majoring in Geology and Entrepreneurship. She is a clay artist and serves on the Cowee Pottery School Board of Directors.

Molly spends her free time backwoods hiking, baking fresh-picked mountain blueberry pies and throwing pots in "the Institute of Mud". She will be watching the solar eclipse with Cowee Sam by her side.

# Acknowledgements

We would like to thank Monica Collier of Red Press Co., for her publishing help, Katie Farris and Kaitie Swedlund for their help on special projects, Glen Swedlund for his proof reading, and Michael Zeiler of GreatAmericanEclipse.com for his generosity in letting us use his amazing graphics and pictures.

Special thanks to the real Farmer Joe and Jamy and Jerome and Annie for their love and support.

And most of all, thanks to our heavenly Father for His goodness and love.

Katie Farris and
Kaitie Swedlund

Monica Collier

Glen Swedlund

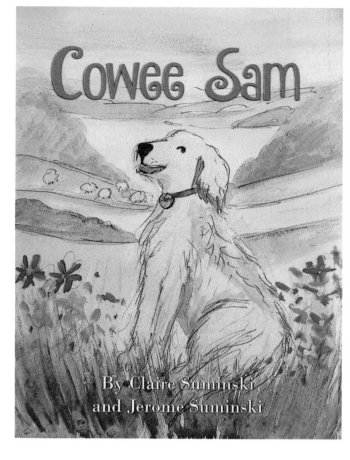

ISBN 9780979386978 56 pages   $14.95 Retail

ISBN 9780979386985 59 pages   $14.95 Retail

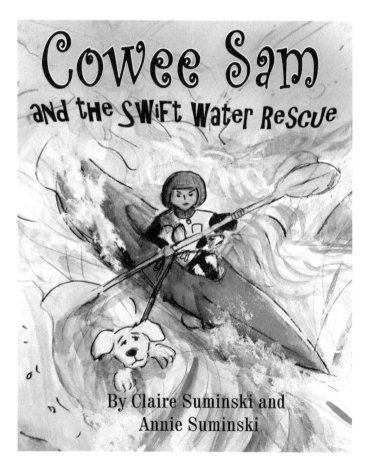

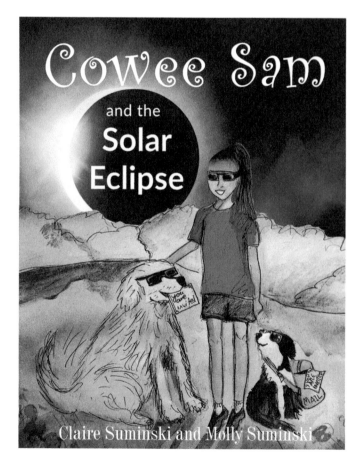

ISBN 9780979386992 58 pages   $14.95 Retail

SuminskiFamilyBooks.com

CPSIA information can be obtained
at www.ICGtesting.com
Printed in the USA
LVOW05s0115130717
541163LV00006B/8/P